Weekly Reader Children's Book Club presents

FREDERICK'S ALLIGATOR

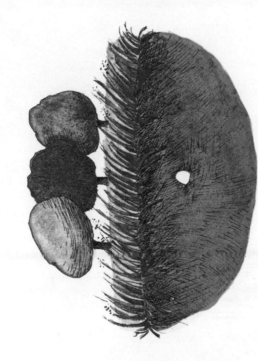

ESTHER ALLEN PETERSON

FREDERICK'S ALLIGATOR

ILLUSTRATED BY SUSANNA NATTI

CROWN PUBLISHERS, INC., NEW YORK

Text copyright © 1979 by Esther Allen Peterson
Illustrations copyright © 1979 by Susanna Natti

The text of this book is set in 14 point Bookman. The illustrations are black half-tone
drawings, with half-tone overlays, prepared by the artist, for red and yellow.

Library of Congress Cataloging in Publication Data
Peterson, Esther Allen. Frederick's alligator. Summary: Frederick has always
claimed to have wild animals in his house. Then one day he really does become the owner
of a baby alligator. [1. Alligators—Fiction. 2. Imagination—Fiction] I. Natti, Susanna.
II. Title. PZ7.P4434Fr [E] 78-15597 ISBN 0-517-53597-1

For Paul,
who has lions in his closet

One morning Frederick said to his mom, "I have a pet lion in my closet. We are pals, and he will eat you up if you ever spank me."

"Sure, Frederick," said his mom. "Now finish your breakfast or you will be late for school."

As Frederick was leaving for school, he saw the mailman coming up the sidewalk. "I have a timber wolf in my basement," he said. "He likes to eat mailmen, so be very careful if you go into our house."

"Sure, Frederick," said the mailman. "Why don't you put his name on the mailbox?"

When Frederick got to school, he said, "I have a grizzly bear in my attic. He can tear a man or beast into a hundred pieces in just one minute."

"Sure, Frederick," said his teacher. "Now *please* take your seat."

That day on the way home from school, Frederick went to the river to look for wild animals. But all he found was a dead fish, an egg sticking out of the mud, and an old shoe box.

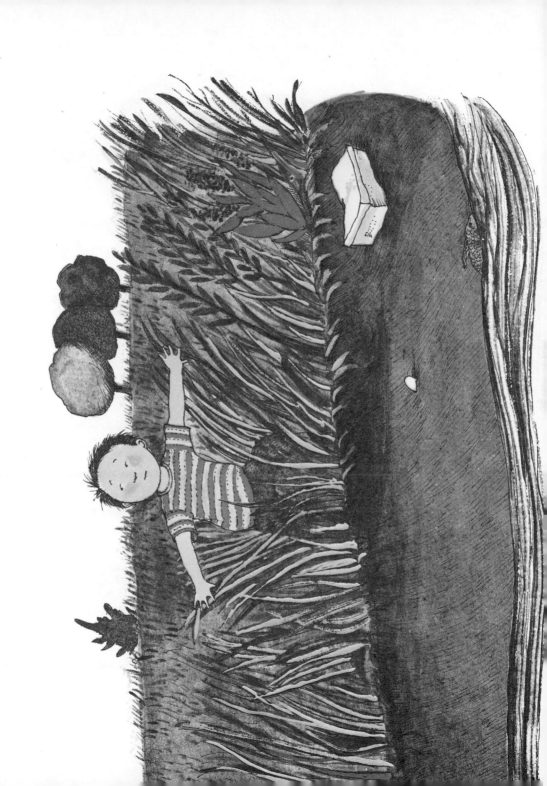

He put the egg in the shoe box and packed it with mud and leaves. Then he carried it home and hid it under his bed.

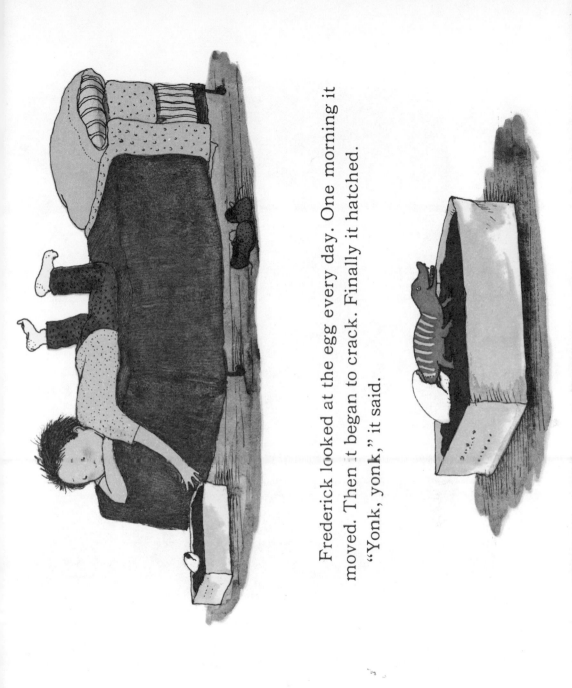

Frederick looked at the egg every day. One morning it moved. Then it began to crack. Finally it hatched. "Yonk, yonk," it said.

When Frederick put the alligator on the floor, it yawned.
Then it tried out its wobbly legs.

Frederick put the alligator in a pan of water, hid it under his bed, and went downstairs.

"I have a baby alligator under my bed," said Frederick. "That's nice," said his mom. "I hope your lion doesn't eat it."

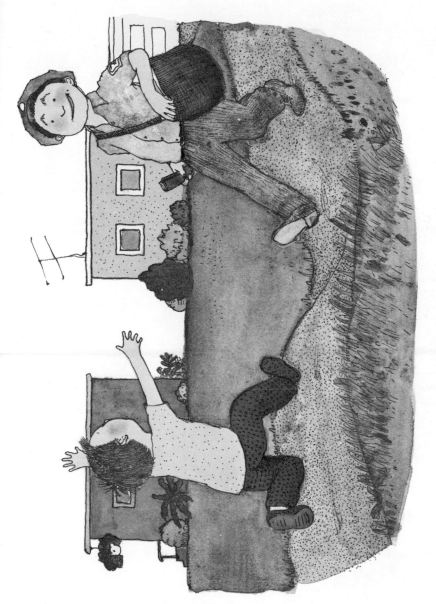

On the way to school Frederick saw the mailman. "I
have a baby alligator under my bed."

"That's nice," said the mailman. "Now your timber wolf
has a playmate."

When Frederick arrived at school he said, "I have a baby alligator under my bed. Can I bring him for show-and-tell?"

"Sure, Frederick," said his teacher. "And bring your grizzly bear, too."

The next morning Frederick put his alligator in the shoe box and carried it downstairs.

"Frederick!" said his mom. "You *do* have an alligator!"

"I sure do," he said. "And teacher said I can bring it for show-and-tell."

On the way to school they met the mailman. "Frederick!"
he said. "You *do* have an alligator!"

"I sure do," said Frederick.

When they got to school, everyone said, "Frederick! You *do* have an alligator!"

That morning at show-and-tell, Frederick said, "I found an alligator egg in the riverbank, and I took it home and put it under my bed until it hatched. He eats bugs, worms, and cat food."

The teacher said, "Frederick, please put your alligator on the back table with the science projects."

At noon the alligator was missing. The tadpoles and the silkworms were missing, too.

The children looked under their seats and in the wastepaper basket, but Frederick's alligator was nowhere to be found.

Frederick worried all afternoon.

At the end of the day Frederick's best friend was putting on his boots. "Here it is!" he shouted.

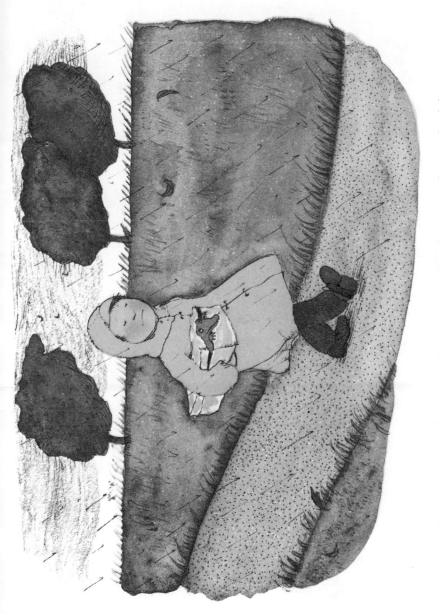

Frederick put his alligator in the box and carried it home. "I don't think I should keep you," he said. "When you get bigger, you might eat my hamster...or even my baby brother."

Frederick tied his alligator to a tree in front of his house. But no one wanted to buy it. Not the mailman, nor the neighbors, nor anyone on the street.

Frederick thought and thought. Then he untied the
alligator from the tree and carried it back to the riverbank.
"Good-by," he said. "I thought you would be a nice pet.
But I guess I'll stick to hamsters, and maybe even white
mice and garter snakes."

At home his mom didn't think there was a lion in his closet, but she looked anyway.

The mailman wondered if there was a timber wolf in Frederick's basement.

And to this day, his classmates still wonder if there
is a grizzly bear in his attic,

but Frederick won't tell.